PAUL

PAUL
Adventurer for Christ

Written by
GWENDOLYNE
ARBUCKLE

Revised by
CAROLYN
WOLCOTT

Abingdon Press
Nashville

PAUL: ADVENTURER FOR CHRIST

Copyright © 1984 by Abingdon Press

Library of Congress Cataloging in Publication Data

ARBUCKLE, GWENDOLYNE.
  Paul: adventurer for Christ.
  "Originally from *Older Elementary Student*, VCS 1978"—T.p. verso.
  Summary: Describes the life and teaching of the apostle Paul.
  1. Paul, the Apostle, Saint—Juvenile literature.
  2. Christian saints—Turkey—Tarsus—Biography—Juvenile litera-
ture. [1.Paul, the Apostle, Saint. 2. Saints] I. Wolcott, Carolyn M.
(Carolyn Muller) II. Title.
BS2506.5.A67   1984   225.9'24 [B]   83-15620

ISBN 0-687-30487-3

Originally from *Older Elementary Student*, VCS 1978. Copyright ©
1977 by Graded Press.

MANUFACTURED IN THE UNITED STATES OF AMERICA

Contents

Chapter 1/The Adventure
Begins, A. D. 32 7

Chapter 2/The Start of a New
Adventure, A. D. 49 ....*21*

Chapter 3/Adventuring with Tongue
and Pen, A. D. 52 ....*39*

Chapter 4/Adventuring in the Face
of Danger, A. D. 56 ....*57*

Chapter 5/The Adventure
Ends, A. D. 59-61 (or 64) *75*

Chapter 6/An Afterword for Parents
and Teachers *85*

Important Words *91*

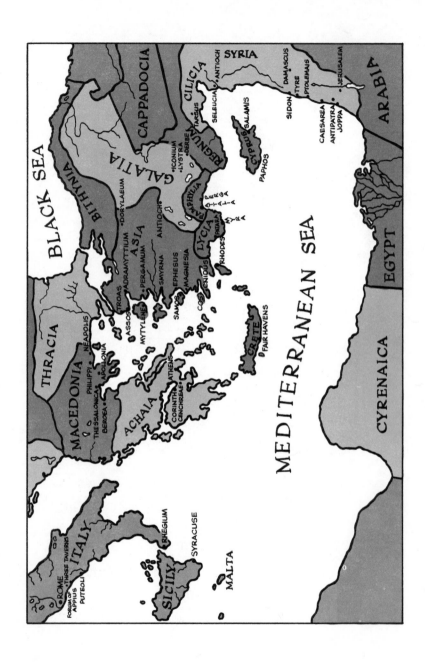

Chapter 1/*The Adventure Begins, A.D. 32*

SAUL, BOY OF TARSUS

Young Saul sat on the floor in front of the loom and folded his feet under him. His father was teaching him to throw the shuttle through the loom. How tired his hands were! The rough goat's hair scratched as he worked it into the heavy-duty cloth known throughout the world as Cilician cloth. Like most small boys he grumbled when he had to work. "Father, why must I make cloth for sails and tents? I want to become a rabbi."

"Ah, my son, you shall become a rabbi even though we live in this Gentile city of Tarsus. But a rabbi must also earn a living. Jews have a saying, 'A father who does not teach his son to work with his hands makes him no better than a thief.' And you, Saul, are not only a Jew, you are a Pharisaic Jew. You can be proud, my son, because Pharisees keep the law of Moses, and all the other Jewish religious laws."

Young Saul of Tarsus worked away at his loom, but his mind was often on the great, holy city of Jerusalem. He wished he could go there and learn from the great rabbis.

Then one day his father announced, "Saul, today we have received a letter from your sister and her family in Jerusalem."

Saul held his breath and looked expectantly at his father.

"Yes, Saul, you are to go and live with her and study in the temple with the great Gamaliel."

It seemed everybody had advice and plans for Saul! But it was his father who said over and over during the next few weeks. "Saul, life will be very different in Jerusalem. Saul, stand firm in your faith."

"I know, Father," promised Saul. "I am a Pharisee. I will live strictly by the law of our people."

SAUL, STUDENT IN JERUSALEM

Young, eager, enthusiastic, reared in a strict background, the student Saul did just what might be expected when he arrived in Jerusalem at the age of eighteen. He put all his energy into keeping the religious law.

It was easy enough until Stephen came into the picture. Stephen was an outstanding young member of the Greek-speaking synagogue in Jerusalem and an enthusiastic follower of Jesus. He went among the Greek-speaking Jews asking them to become followers of Jesus' Way. Some Jews who were jealous of Stephen said he was speaking against God. They brought him before the Council—the rulers of the Jewish temple—and questioned him. Stephen told the Council, "Your forefathers never paid any attention to forward-looking prophets. And you acted in the same way as your ancestors when you killed Jesus." Then, looking up, he cried, "I can see Jesus standing at God's right hand."

This was too much for the Council. They rushed at Stephen, dragged him out of the city, and stoned him to death. Just before he died, Stephen cried out, "Lord, do not hold this sin against them."

Saul witnessed the killing of Stephen. He did not throw any stones, but he approved of the murder and minded the coats of those who stoned him.

SAUL, PERSECUTOR

Saul threw himself energetically into searching house after house, seizing men and women who were Jesus' followers, and sending them off to prison. He even asked the high priest to give him authority to go to the city of Damascus to arrest the followers of Jesus in that city.

But something happened on that road to Damascus. Saul rode proudly along accompanied by his bodyguard. Was he thinking of the way Stephen's face had glowed as he prayed for those who were putting him to death? Suddenly a light flashed in the sky and seemed to wrap itself around Saul. Saul fell to the ground and heard a voice saying, "Saul, Saul, why do you persecute me?"

"Who are you, Lord?" gasped Saul.

And the voice answered, "I am Jesus, whom you are persecuting."

When Saul stood up, he was blind. He had started out like a conqueror going to take a city, but now he had to be led to Damascus.

In Damascus God sent to Saul a man named Ananias. Ananias was a follower of Jesus. He had heard about Saul. Everything he had heard had made him afraid of this man. It took courage for him to go to the house on Straight Street where Saul was staying. But when he saw Saul's blindness, he was filled with compassion. He laid his hands on Saul and prayed. Immediately Saul could see again.

SAUL, THE PERSECUTED

Right away Saul asked to be baptized. He started going to the synagogue of Damascus and preaching. Now he was preaching that Jesus was the Son of God, the very thing for which he had been persecuting the followers of Jesus. Now he was urging the Jews to follow Jesus just as energetically as he had once persecuted those who had.

The Jews did not like what he was saying, especially that Jesus was the Son of God, the Messiah for whom Jews had been looking for centuries. They plotted to kill Saul.

Saul left Damascus as dramatically as he entered it. He escaped one night by being lowered in a basket from a window in the city wall, let down in the dark of night!

We are not quite sure what Paul did after this. Later he wrote to the Christians in Galatia that as soon as he was converted he went to Arabia and then returned to Damascus.

But the Book of Acts says that he immediately set out for Jerusalem to see Cephas (Peter). In Jerusalem the disciples were doubtful. Some did not believe that Saul had changed. The Jews looked on him as a deserter and hated him. So again Saul had to escape.

This time it was Barnabas, one of Jesus' followers, who came to the rescue. His name meant "son of encouragement." He helped Saul escape to Caesarea and suggested that he go back home to Tarsus.

Saul went home. He worked on the cloth until his hands hurt. He sold tents to Roman soldiers, awnings to Greek merchants, and sails to Phoenician seamen. He taught in the synagogue and talked to people in the marketplace. Saul found the Greeks to be his most eager students. Meanwhile, followers of Jesus' Way were so badly treated in Jerusalem that they moved out to Cyprus, Phoenicia, and Syria. Antioch, the capital of Syria, became a great center for them. It was in Antioch that the followers of Jesus were first called Christians—Christ-ones—by people who wanted to make fun of them.

Barnabas was working among the Christians in Antioch. He found he couldn't handle it alone. He needed help. Barnabas remembered Saul in Tarsus, and went to find him. He brought Saul back to Antioch, and for a whole year they worked with the church there and taught about Jesus.

One day a prophet named Agabus came from Jerusalem to Antioch. He predicted that a great famine was coming. The disciples in Antioch decided to take an offering to help the

Christians in Jerusalem and to send Saul and Barnabas to Jerusalem with their gifts.

Ten years had passed since Saul's last visit to Jerusalem and his hurried escape. Many changes had taken place. Herod Agrippa I was now king. In order to win the favor of the Jews, he persecuted the Christians. James, the brother of John, had been beheaded. Peter (Cephas) had been arrested but had escaped from jail. Saul was glad when he and Barnabas were safely out of Jerusalem and on their way back to Antioch.

Barnabas' cousin, John Mark, a young Christian in whose home Jesus had often visited, went to Antioch with them.

Soon these three men had new travel plans. The church at Antioch set Saul and Barnabas apart as missionaries and sent them to far places to tell the story of Jesus.

LAND-HO

The little open-decked ship with its brightly colored square sail hoisted to the wind crept carefully across the brilliant blue Mediterranean Sea.

The lookout spotted the eastern-most tip of the island of Cyprus. As the ship glided into the harbor of Salamis on the southern shore, Barnabas could hide his excitement no longer. "Saul, it is good to be home! We will visit with my family, then follow the coastal road to Paphos, the Roman capital of this island."

About this time, Saul became known by his own Roman name, Paul.

Paul and his company sailed from Paphos to the province of Pamphylia, a tiny country made up of a narrow strip between the towering Taurus Mountains and the Mediterranean Sea. They landed at Attalia and went on foot to Perga, a city famous for pagan worship places.

John Mark left Paul and Barnabas in Perga—perhaps he was homesick. He returned to Jerusalem, but Paul and Barnabas continued on their journey.

A LONG HIKE

Paul and Barnabas set off alone on the road which followed the Cestrus River Valley. Leaving the valley, the road suddenly became rough and steep. This one-hundred-mile road was famous for robbers. At places it was little more than a mountain trail. Sometimes it crossed swift rivers. Food had to be found along the way. It took Paul and Barnabas more than two weeks to reach the fertile plain on which Pisidian Antioch was built.

On the Sabbath they went to the synagogue, as they always did. After the Scripture reading, the rulers invited Paul and the other visitors to speak.

"My brothers," Paul began, "the people of Jerusalem and their leaders did not understand the words of the old-time prophets which we read every Sabbath Day. But they made the words come true by having Pilate put Jesus to death, even though there was no legal reason to do so. But God raised him from the dead, and he was seen by many of his disciples. They are now witnesses for him to the people of Israel. And we are here to bring the Good News to you!"

The next Sabbath, it seemed as if the whole city had come to hear Paul and Barnabas.

Unfortunately, not everybody was pleased with what they heard. When the strict Jews saw the crowd of Gentile Christians, they became jealous of Paul.

Paul boldly answered his critics, "It was necessary to tell you first about God's word, but if you do not believe me, then we will turn to the Gentiles."

The Gentiles were pleased to hear this, and they began to spread the news everywhere. The strict Jews were not pleased and stirred up a riot.

STALKED BY TROUBLE

Once more Paul was on the run. He and Barnabas "shook the dust off their feet" and walked eighty or ninety miles southeast to Iconium, in Galatia. Paul and Barnabas stayed a long time in Iconium, and there were many conversions. But the longer they stayed, the more the Jews and the Gentiles argued with each other. Finally, both sides became so angry that they tried to stone Paul and Barnabas. They barely escaped!

After a six-hour hike to the south, they reached Lystra, a city of Lycaonia. They found few Jews in Lystra and no synagogue at all. There was nothing for them to do but preach directly to the Gentiles in the marketplace.

Soon trouble followed in the form of Jews from the synagogues in Pisidian Antioch and Iconium. They stoned Paul and dragged him outside the city and left him for dead. But when his friends came, he was able to get up and walk back into the city. Paul explained to his amazed friends, "It was God who took care of me because he has called me for a mission which I have not accomplished."

On the run again, Paul and Barnabas left Lystra for Derbe, forty miles away. Derbe was also a Lycaonian city, half Greek, half Oriental, but even here a group of believers was soon formed.

Paul and Barnabas were not bothered here by the strict Jews from Pisidian Antioch and

Iconium who were willing to chase them one day's journey, but not two.

One day, Barnabas remarked to Paul, "If we continue traveling as we have been, we will soon come again to Tarsus and Antioch in Syria."

"Yes," answered Paul, "I would like to visit my family in Tarsus and then get back to our brothers in Antioch."

However, both men realized they could not do it! They knew the Christians in the cities they had left were discouraged and needed help.

So Paul and Barnabas headed back to the places from which they had barely escaped!

Their friends were delighted to see them again. As Paul and Barnabas kept on preaching, more and more Gentiles became believers of the Way. They began to organize the followers into a permanent church.

The missionaries appointed elders, teachers, bishops, and deacons to keep the churches going after the missionaries left.

From Pisidian Antioch, they came to the coast of Perga where they were able to preach for the first time. Paul and Barnabas turned westward to the port of Attalia and from there sailed down the coast to their own home church in Syrian Antioch.

Their missionary journey of more than two years was completed! They had traveled about fourteen hundred miles, half by sea and half by land, and now were eager to report to the church in Antioch.

All this—Paul's first missionary journey— took place about the years A.D. 45–47.

Chapter 2/*The Start of a New Adventure,* A.D. *49*

REPORT TO THE CHURCH

Two whole years had passed by the time Paul and Barnabas returned to Antioch in Syria. The whole church gathered to hear the report from their traveling missionaries.

Paul and Barnabas told of the trip through Cyprus where they had met many friendly people, about John Mark leaving them, about the hard trip up the mountains to Pisidian Antioch.

Paul told about being beaten in Iconium and stoned by the Judaizers in Pisidian Antioch and Iconium. He then added, "Brothers, think how many Gentiles out in the provinces of the

Empire have accepted the message of our Lord Jesus Christ!"

Even in Antioch the old question of strictly keeping the Law kept coming up. Must a person first become a Jew before he could become a Christian? There was nothing to do but settle it with the apostles and elders in the Jerusalem church. Who could present the Gentile side better than Paul and Barnabas? They would go to Jerusalem and talk with the church leaders there. They would take with them Titus, a Greek convert in Antioch whose life was an example of the Christian Way.

OFF TO JERUSALEM

So Paul, Barnabas, Titus, and some others went to Jerusalem to meet with the leaders of the church.

Paul told of the things God had done among the Gentiles and through him and Barnabas. He said, "The old prophets spoke of the inwardness of religion, and they said ceremonies and sacrifices were of little importance. It is only in recent years that our religion has become so completely caught up in demands for legal details."

The Judaizers were horrified and alarmed. Such talk was wild! But Paul went on, "God wants the Gentiles to be saved only by their faith."

Cephas, who was also called Peter, his Greek name, stood up and told once more about the vision he had years before in Joppa. In this vision God had said to him, "Whatever I have made clean, you shall count clean!" He concluded, "We believe we shall be saved through the grace of the Lord Jesus and so will the Gentiles."

The debate was long. Finally, James, who was Jesus' brother and head of the Jerusalem church said, "Brothers, we should not force the Gentiles who turn to God to follow the Jewish customs. Instead, we should write to them and tell them what we expect of them."

A LETTER TO GENTILE CHRISTIANS

Everyone agreed and so a letter was sent to the Antioch church. It said simply: "Do not eat meat which has been killed as a sacrifice to idols. Do not eat any animal which has been strangled, or in any other way allow blood in your food. And you must not act in wrong ways."

Paul and Barnabas went back to Antioch with the letter and stayed there a few months. Then they were eager to be on the move again, to visit the churches they had started. Barnabas wanted to take John Mark along, but Paul remembered how John Mark had left them three years earlier and refused.

So Barnabas and his young cousin sailed together for Cyprus, and Paul chose a new traveling companion, Silas, whom he always called by his Roman name, Silvanus. They headed north through Syria and on to Cilicia.

Now Paul and Silvanus walked through fertile valleys, crossed a mountain range, ferried across swollen rivers. Along the way they preached, and Paul said time and time again, "Stand firm in your faith." He carried with him a copy of James' letter.

Going through the rough mountain country was difficult. Paul and Silvanus went faster across the dull, unchanging plains. Eventually they came to Derbe. After the hardships of travel and cold nights spent camping out, they were glad for the rest and food they found among their friends in Derbe.

After a few weeks they moved on toward Lystra. There they found Timothy who had been just a boy when Paul was in Lystra

before. What a fine young man he had grown to be. "Timothy," Paul said, "I want you to visit the churches with us."

Timothy was so excited that he wanted to leave that very day! However, Paul and Silvanus wanted time to preach to the church in Lystra. At last the day came when the three friends set out toward the west. They spent a few happy days in Iconium and a little longer in Pisidian Antioch. They went through the region of Phrygia and Galatia almost to the borders of Mysia. At this point they went to the city of Troas. Perhaps it was because Paul was ill, and because they had heard that a physician was in Troas that they went there. At any rate, they met Luke, the physician, and this meeting developed into a life-long friendship between Luke and Paul. Luke took care of Paul, and Paul shared the Good News about Christ.

A STRANGE DREAM

One night, while they were in Troas, Paul had a dream. In his dream, he saw a man from Macedonia with his arms outstretched, begging, "Come, come over into Macedonia and help us."

Right away Paul looked for a ship to take him and his companions to Macedonia. They landed at the harbor town of Neapolis. From there they walked the Roman road ten miles to the city of Philippi. Paul looked down the road and knew it ran on to the faraway shores of the Adriatic Sea. Maybe, someday, he could sail the Adriatic Sea to Italy and pick up the road that led on to the great city of Rome.

Paul shook his head to clear it of his daydreams. He had just set foot on European soil! God had led him there to tell the people that Jesus is the Messiah. He must keep his eye on the goal.

As they passed through the gates of Philippi, Paul noticed the busy marketplace. He did not see a synagogue and was disappointed to learn that there were only a few Jews in Philippi.

When the Sabbath came, Paul thought, *I know where I can find the Jews worshiping. They will be near a stream of water where they can wash their hands before praying.*

Paul walked about a mile and a half out of town and found a small group of women worshiping God along a river bank. The women welcomed him with curiosity. Then he preached to them about Jesus. He told them how Jesus had been killed and then rose from the dead. "And," said Paul, "you and I can win over death by simply believing that God's grace is enough for us."

Lydia, a businesswoman who sold purple cloth, said, "Paul, I would like my whole household to be baptized in this new faith."

Paul's converts in Philippi formed a church that met in Lydia's house on the first day of the week. They listened to the reading of the Scriptures. They sang hymns, offered prayers, and listened to Paul preach.

JAIL AGAIN

One day as Paul and Silvanus walked through the streets, they were followed by a slave girl who told fortunes to make money for her masters. For several days she followed Paul and his friends around teasing them about being servants of the most high God. Finally, Paul, annoyed, turned to her and said, "Evil spirit, in the name of Jesus Christ come out of her."

The slave girl's owners were so angry they grabbed Paul and Silvanus and dragged them before the magistrates—the rulers of the city. The magistrates ordered Paul and Silvanus beaten and thrown in jail. That night the city was rocked by a great earthquake. The whole building shook. The doors flew open. Even the chains on the prisoners' legs were broken. The jailer feared all the prisoners had escaped and he was about to kill himself.

"Stop," called Paul. "Nobody has escaped."

The astonished jailer fell down before Paul and Silvanus. "What can I do to be saved?" he asked.

Paul and Silvanus answered, "Believe in the Lord, and you will be saved, you and your whole household." The jailer and his whole household were baptized in the Christian faith.

The next day the magistrates sent word to release Paul and Silvanus, but Paul said, "Let them come and face us themselves. They have illegally beaten us, we who are Roman citizens."

RUN OUT OF TOWN

When the magistrates heard that Paul and Silvanus were Roman citizens, they hurried to the jail, apologized, and asked them to leave town quickly.

But first Paul and Silvanus went to the home of Lydia to say good-bye to the new Christians who were waiting there for news of them. Paul left Luke in Philippi, probably to look after the church there, and he, Silvanus, and Timothy left Philippi by way of the western gate.

TURNING THE WORLD UPSIDE DOWN

It was noon when Paul, Silvanus, and Timothy left Philippi. Four days later they were at Thessalonica, the capital of Macedonia.

The busy streets in the heart of the city were crowded with caravans loaded with every kind of goods. The shopkeepers were from many nations. Roman soldiers and officials were everywhere.

Silvanus decided that Thessalonica would serve as a center from which the gospel would be carried in all directions.

Paul said, "Let's find the synagogue. We will go there first thing to meet the Jews in the city."

Never had Paul been more eagerly welcomed. Each time he spoke, people crowded into the synagogue to listen. More and more came to believe that Jesus of Nazareth was the Messiah they had been waiting for for so long. Most of the converts were Jews, but some were outstanding Greek men and women who believed, too.

To support himself and Timothy and Silvanus, Paul worked at his trade of tentmaking. The church in Philippi sent some money which helped.

Silvanus' prediction that the gospel would go in all directions from Thessalonica was correct. The new Christians spread the word about Jesus, the Messiah, throughout Macedonia. Suddenly Paul was famous.

Now the strict Jews became jealous and upset. They gathered together some rabble-rousers and started a riot. They knew the missionaries had stayed in the home of a man named Jason, so they went there searching for Paul. When they didn't find Paul in Jason's house, they dragged Jason and some other converts off to the town magistrates and reported, "These are the men who have turned the world upside down. We know that Caesar is our king. These people are saying there is another king whose name is Jesus."

The magistrates were afraid of a Jewish riot, so they made Jason and the others post bond before they let them go.

The Christians were afraid Paul might be killed, so they hurried Paul and Timothy and Silvanus off to Berea about forty miles southwest of Thessalonica.

In Berea the synagogues were opened to
them and the people welcomed them eagerly.
Many Jews and Greeks, both men and women,
were converted. Paul was pleased.

Then it happened again. Some of the Jews of
Thessalonica came down to Berea to stir up the
people against Paul. The Christians in Berea
decided they should get Paul out of town as fast
as possible. Paul left for Athens, but he left
Timothy and Silvanus behind to strengthen the
faith of the new converts.

THE LEARNED CITY

In Athens, Paul walked through the streets
all alone among the thousands of people in this
great city. Athens had long been a center of
learning. In the city were famous schools,
temples, and statues of gods and goddesses.

Paul was not impressed by the temples and
statues because they were built for pagan
worship. He used every chance he had in the
agora—the Greek marketplace—and in the synagogue to tell people about Jesus and the
resurrection. The Athenian scholars invited him
to Mars Hill, a short distance from the agora.
There Paul spoke to the most outstanding and
best-educated leaders of Athens. He said, "Men

of Athens, I notice that you are very religious. I have seen your many altars. I even saw one with a sign 'To an Unknown God.' You have been worshiping him, and now I am going to tell you who he is."

Paul talked to them about God and about Jesus. But when he said that Jesus, after he had been put to death rose from the dead, many of the Athenians made fun of Paul.

A few people had second thoughts, however, and came back to ask Paul more questions. Some believed and were converted. Among them was a man of high social position named Dionysius, and a woman named Damaris.

After that not much happened in Athens, and Paul moved on to Corinth, forty miles away.

THE WICKED CITY

What a city Corinth was! In the harbor were ships from every nation. Cargo included silver, copper, iron, pottery, glass, dyed cloth, leather, jewelry, grain, fruit—every item of commerce. What a noisy, smelly, busy place it was, and what an assortment of people—sailors, merchants, refugees, criminals—every race, speaking every language. Corinth was said to be the most wicked city in the Roman Empire. Paul knew there was plenty to do in Corinth.

But his first task was to find work, to earn his own living. He walked down the crowded streets of the business district with the few tools of the tentmaker's trade in his travel bag. Almost immediately he found a tentmaker who had recently come to Corinth and set up his shop. And to Paul's surprise and delight he found that this man, Aquila, and his wife Priscilla (sometimes called Prisca) were Christian Jews. They had been forced to leave Rome when Emperor Claudius deported all Jews from that city. They were equally delighted to find that Paul was a fellow Christian. They invited him to live with them and to work in their shop.

On the Sabbath, Paul went with Priscilla and Aquila to the synagogue. As a stranger, he was invited to speak to the congregation after the reading of the Scripture. He spoke very simply about the crucifixion and the resurrection of Christ. The households of Stephanas, Crispus, and Gaius were the first converts of Corinth. Paul baptized them.

What a happy day it was when Silvanus and Timothy arrived—and with good news from the Christians in Philippi and Thessalonica! They had stood firm in their faith!

But history repeated itself. The strict Jews would not listen to anything Paul had to say about Jesus being the Messiah. Finally, Paul took all he could of their bickering. He shook out his robe to show that he would have nothing more to do with them and announced, "From now on I will preach to the Gentiles."

After that he stayed with Titus Justus, a Gentile who worshiped God and lived next door to the synagogue. But Crispus, the leader of the synagogue, believed what Paul said, and he and all his household, along with many other Corinthians, were baptized.

Still, plots and quarrels and feuds went on all around Paul while he was preaching the gospel of peace and love! Sometimes he wondered if he were making matters worse because his preaching brought out such anger in so many people.

For all his great courage, the constant threats against his life discouraged him. One night, however, he dreamed that God said to him, "Do not be afraid to speak out plainly. I am with you and no one is going to harm you."

Paul stayed in Corinth a year and six months. The time came for him to leave. Not only Silvanus and Timothy, but also Aquila and Priscilla left with him. The men of the Corinthian congregation walked with them to the edge of the city. Saying good-bye was hard for all of them!

Aquila and Priscilla took all their household goods with them, for they were moving to Ephesus.

When the ship docked at Ephesus more good-byes were said. The ship sailed on, south and east, and brought Paul, Silvanus, and Timothy to Caesarea. Paul made a quick trip to

Jerusalem, then hurried on to Antioch in Syria to report to the Antioch church on his three-year-long journey. The year was about A.D. 51 and Paul's second missionary journey was at an end.

Chapter 3/*Adventuring with Tongue and Pen*, A.D. 52

OFF ON A THIRD JOURNEY

The church in Antioch was eager to hear about Paul's second missionary journey, and Paul was eager to report.

News kept trickling in from here and there in Galatia that the Judaizers were at work. They had taken advantage of Paul's three-year absence to stir up the Gentiles over the old question of whether it was necessary to become a Jew, before becoming Christian.

So off Paul went by the overland route to visit the churches in Galatia and Phrygia—in the cities of Derbe, Lystra, Iconium, Pisidian Antioch—to set the converts straight again.

This time Titus went with him. Timothy had gone home to his family in Lystra in the fall when they had arrived in Antioch. He was to join Paul and Titus in Lystra. Paul, in his haste to get to the "regions of Galatia and Phrygia," bypassed his own family and friends in Tarsus.

Paul revisited all the churches he had started, but he did not stay more than a few weeks in any one of them. He and his companions passed through Colossae and Laodicea on their way to Ephesus.

They arrived in Ephesus in late summer of A.D. 53.

A SPLENDID CITY

Ephesus was a splendid city, the capital and main port of Asia. Asia was the richest province of the Roman Empire. Among the cities of the Empire, Ephesus ranked fourth after Rome, Alexandria, and Antioch in Syria.

Ephesus was a city of beautiful buildings. But its grand landmark was the gigantic temple of Artemis, the most popular goddess.

Paul, in a hurry to get to Aquila and Priscilla, hardly glanced at the beautiful buildings. He joined his friends in the tentmaking shop next to their home. They talked for hours. Paul told

them everything that had happened to him
since they had left the ship in Ephesus. Aquila
and Priscilla had worked faithfully in the
synagogue, and they, too, had much good news
to share. They also had some not-so-good news
for Paul.

Faster than Paul could travel came the news
that the Judaizers were stirring up the
churches in Galatia again, saying that Paul was
not a true apostle. Who was he, they said, to
accept Christians into the Christian fellowship
without requiring them to follow the old Jewish
Law? After all, they said, he was taking his
orders from the real apostles in the Jerusalem
church! Christian salvation, they felt, was the
exclusive right of the Jewish people and could
be had only on their terms.

Such teaching, Paul knew, would crush the
spark of life of the Galatian Christians. It would
make Christianity just a system of rules and
regulations, harsh, narrow, exclusive, with no
room for the joy and love which were the real
spirit of Christ.

A SCOLDING LETTER

Paul dictated a letter addressed "to the
churches in Galatia." He meant for it to be

passed around and read aloud in Derbe, Lystra, Iconium, Pisidian Antioch, and the other churches in the province of Galatia.

Without his usual warm greeting, Paul lashed out at his friends: "Foolish Galatians! Are you hypnotized? Or bewitched? You used to understand the meaning of Jesus Christ's death perfectly well as I explained it to you. Let me ask you this: Did you receive the Holy Spirit by keeping the Jewish laws or by hearing with faith? If you did not first receive the Spirit through the laws, what makes you think that keeping the laws will make you stronger Christians?

"Why did God give the laws? To show what wrongdoing is. Are God's laws and God's promises against each other? Of course not! Until Christ came, the law was the only guide and teacher we had; it controlled us. Now we are sons of God, and Christ controls us through our faith.

"We are no longer Jews or Greeks or slaves or free men and women, but we are all the same—we are Christians; we are one in Christ Jesus. This makes us true children of Abraham and of all God's promises in him.

"Now that God has sent his son to us, we can rightly speak of God as our dear Father.

"Before you Gentiles found God—or I should say before God found you—you were slaves to so-called gods that did not even exist. Do you want to be slaves again to a poor, weak, useless religion of trying to get to heaven by obeying God's laws?"

Paul remembered how warmly the Galatians received him on his first visit, and he reminded them of this. He wrote, "When I first came to you, you were warm and friendly toward me. Even though I was sick, you took me in. Why, you would have taken out your eyes and given them to replace mine if that would have helped me. Where is your old happy spirit? What has happened?"

Paul wrote angrily about the Judaizers: "They are false teachers trying to shut you off from me so you will give them a lot of attention." He reminded them of something he had said once before: "If anyone is preaching to you a gospel different from the one you accepted, let God's curse fall upon him."

He wrote about the Jerusalem Conference in which the leaders of the church had agreed that God had given him, Paul, the task of preaching the gospel to the Gentiles, just as Peter had been given the task of preaching the gospel to the Jews. "The only thing that Peter, James, and John asked," said Paul, "is that we remember to help the poor, and that I was eager to do."

Paul gave the Galatians practical advice. He wrote: "As for you, my brothers, you were called to be free. But do not let this freedom become an excuse for letting your physical desires control you. Instead, let love make you serve one another. For the whole Law is summed up in one commandment: 'Love your neighbor as you love yourself.' . . .

"The Spirit produces love, joy, peace, patience, kindness, goodness, faithfulness, humility, and self-control. There is no law against such things as these. . . .

"Help carry one another's burdens, and in this way you will obey the law of Christ. If someone thinks he is something when he really is nothing, he is only deceiving himself. . . .

"The man who is being taught the Christian message should share all the good things he has with his teacher.

"Do not deceive yourselves; no one makes a fool of God. A person will reap exactly what he plants. . . . So let us not become tired of doing good; for if we do not give up, the time will come when we will reap the harvest. So then, as often as we have the chance, we should do good to everyone, and especially to those who belong to our family in the faith" (Gal. 5:13-14, 22-23; 6:2-3, 6-7, 9-10 TEV).

Paul dictated the letter. Now he added a warning in his own handwriting: "The only thing that counts is whether we become changed into new and different people, through Christ. I don't want to hear again this argument from you, for my body is already scarred with whippings and wounds from Jesus' enemies that mark me as Jesus' slave."

TROUBLE AHEAD

Paul folded and sealed the papyrus roll.

He prayed that the Christians in the Galatian churches would now be able to stand firm, and that he could spend his time building up the church in Ephesus.

But Paul was about to have problems in Ephesus!

Paul spoke in the synagogue every Sabbath and pleaded with the Jews to accept Christ as their hoped-for Messiah. But some were stubborn and refused to believe. Some even said evil things about the Way of Jesus before the whole congregation.

So Paul refused to preach to them any longer. He rented a lecture hall from a man named Tyrannus. Here, for the next two years, he spoke daily and led discussions with the disciples from the synagogue and with anyone who wanted to listen.

God gave Paul power to heal people and to cast out the demons that were troubling them.

Many believers who had not given up their practice of magic confessed. Now they brought their books of charms and burned them at a public bonfire.

Paul tried not to attract public attention. But that bonfire did! It attracted the attention of everyone, especially of a businessman named Demetrius.

THE BIG RIOT

Demetrius was a silversmith. He had a profitable business making silver figures for the goddess Artemis. He called together his fellow workers and said: "Men, you know that we make a good profit from our business. And now, not only here in Ephesus but throughout all Asia, this Paul is persuading people to turn

away from the worship of Artemis. He says
that gods made with hands are not gods. There
is danger that our trade will fall off and that the
temple of the great goddess Artemis—whom all
Asia and the world worship—will count for
nothing."

When they heard this, the silversmiths were
enraged and began to cry out, "Great is
Artemis of the Ephesians."

Running and yelling wildly, they went
through the streets and toward the theater,
dragging with them two of Paul's traveling
companions, Gaius and Aristarchus.

Paul heard the noise and thought he should
go into the crowd to rescue his friends, but the

other disciples stopped him. Even some of the officials of the town, who were Paul's friends, sent word that he must not risk his life by going into the theater.

The scene in the theater was madness! Most of the people did not even know what was going on, but they kept right on shouting, "Great is Artemis of the Ephesians." For two hours more they kept shouting.

Finally, the town clerk was able to quiet the crowd enough so he could be heard. He said, "Men of Ephesus, everybody knows that this city is the temple keeper of the great Artemis. You brought here men who have done or said nothing against Artemis. If, therefore, Demetrius and the silversmiths have a complaint against anyone, let him go through the legal channels. Otherwise, the matter will be settled in the regular meeting of the city council.

"You have risked being charged by the Roman government with a riot today, and I would not know how to explain it." With that warning, he dismissed the crowd, and they scattered.

But they did not forget the incident! From that time on Paul knew he had enemies in Ephesus.

PROBLEMS, PROBLEMS

In the midst of all the troubles in Ephesus, Paul learned that the Corinthian Christians were slipping back into their old pagan ways of living. When Paul was there, he kept everything straightened out. He had promised to come back, but it had been a long time, and he had not returned. The Corinthian Christians were wondering whether he ever would come again. They were forgetting his teachings. Some of them felt that what Paul had taught was too difficult to live by.

A LETTER OF ADVICE

Once more Paul felt that his work was falling apart. Yet he dared not leave Ephesus at this time, because too much depended on him there. Instead, he wrote a letter and sent it to Corinth.

In this first letter to the Corinthian Christians, Paul told the believers to keep away from immoral people who dragged them back to paganism.

Besides writing a letter, Paul sent Timothy to the Corinthian church.

But the situation in Corinth was too difficult for Timothy to handle. The church had split into groups, all arguing, and each group thinking it was right and the others wrong. They were so busy quarreling that they were forgetting to pray, forgetting even the reason for their quarrels, and finding it easy to take up again the pagan life they had left.

At last the Corinthian Christians decided to send a special delegation to Paul to ask him some questions, get his advice, and, and if possible, to persuade him to come in person.

Paul had heard about the troubles in Corinth. Apollos, a leader in the Corinthian church, may have been the cause of some of the trouble without meaning to be. He had been preaching and teaching in his own way. And of course his way was not the same as Paul's since he was a different kind of person.

Some of the Corinthian believers liked his way better than Paul's and said so, even calling themselves "Apollos' party." Others said, "No, Paul is better." Still others knew that Peter was the chief of the apostles, and so they said, "We're for Peter." But some of them thought another way. "We're for Christ," they said, and they would not listen to any teachers at all. And so divisions arose among the people.

Besides all this, many of the believers were behaving in bad ways, living like pagans, and getting drunk, even when they celebrated the Lord's Supper. They were excited about the visions and "spiritual gifts" that came to some believers. But in the middle of all the quarrels and bad behavior, none of the gifts really helped make people holy.

They had forgotten the new life in Christ that Paul had tried to show them!

Now the delegation arrived in Ephesus. The letter they brought raised many new questions: What about marriage and divorce? Was it all right to buy meat in the market of pagan temples? How must women dress for worship? What about spiritual gifts? How should they deal with people who spoke "in tongues"? Could they be sure of the resurrection?

A LETTER WITH A POEM

Paul dictated a letter to the church at Corinth, one of the longest letters he ever sent. He condemned divisions in the church and every slip from the highest standards of Christian conduct. He answered each question that had been asked. He wrote a beautiful poem about Christian love. He made it plain that what people do is worth nothing if they do not really love others. He wrote about the importance of Christ's resurrection. Then he added: "We live first in a physical body, but we also have a 'spiritual body' which will be saved through Christ's resurrection."

Timothy went back to Corinth with the delegation. Before long he was back in Ephesus with a report, and it was more bad news.

Timothy had been met with only insults. The quarrels and arguments which Paul's letter was supposed to end were just as bad. Some people were saying, as the false teachers in Galatia had said, that Paul was no true apostle, just an "upstart" trying to make himself important! Paul was deeply hurt, not because of this insult to himself, but because if the Corinthians hated him they would also hate his teachings, and this teaching was God's message and their salvation.

Paul realized there was nothing to do but go to Corinth himself, although he knew that his absence would give his enemies in Ephesus the chance they had been waiting for.

After a three-day trip by boat, Paul arrived in Corinth, hoping to help the parties make peace. He might as well have met a wall! One

man in particular stirred up many of the people
to disobey Paul. Given time, Paul might have
won back the straying Christians.

But he did not have time. He had to go back
to Ephesus. So he promised his faithful converts that he would come back to Corinth as
soon as possible and stay longer. He sailed to
Ephesus with a heavy heart.

Just as he feared, his enemies had used his
absence to stir up feelings against him in
Ephesus. In the midst of all his troubles, Paul
wrote a third letter to the Corinthians. (It is
also found in II Corinthians.)

A SORROWFUL LETTER

This letter was an angry and sorrowful letter.
He wrote angrily about the people who questioned his authority, who claimed they were the
true Jews, the true apostles and servants of
Christ.

Titus took this letter to Corinth. He was able
to return and meet Paul in Troas, from where
they planned to go together to Macedonia.
Timothy and Erastus were to meet them in
Macedonia in a few weeks.

But things were uneasy in Ephesus. The city
was still upset over the silversmiths' riot

against the church, and the believers begged Paul, for his own safety, to leave at once.

Paul set out for Troas. Titus was not yet there. Paul couldn't stand the delay. He kept remembering the things he had said in his letter. Had he been too harsh? Would the Corinthians behave worse if they were angered? What would they do to Titus? Did they think Paul no longer cared about them? Suppose they lost faith altogether? Would it be his fault?

Paul could not take the suspense sitting still! Although he could see plenty of work to do in Troas, he went on to Macedonia.

There was trouble in Macedonia, too. "Quarrels outside, misgivings inside," as Paul referred to it. Paul was more discouraged than he had ever been because the churches he had started seemed to be in a big mess. But Paul did not lose heart. He could still say, "We are always of good courage."

GOOD NEWS

Then Titus caught up with him. And the news this time was good! Paul's love that would not give up in spite of all they had done had come through to the people. The Corinthians were deeply sorry for what they had done. They turned on the man who had led them against Paul and refused to have anything to do with him. They waited hopefully for Paul's next visit.

A LETTER OF JOY

In his relief and joy, Paul sent Titus back to Corinth with another letter, this one written from Thessalonica. This letter made up for the angry one he had sent before. For the Corinthian church, it must have been almost as good as a visit from Paul.

Paul was eager to put everything right with the Corinthians. Even the man who had been the chief cause of the trouble must be forgiven.

Paul was pleased and relieved because his dear, foolish Corinthians were once more in love and faith. "I am so proud of you that in spite of all our troubles here, I am overjoyed," he wrote.

Paul's four letters to the Christians in Corinth are found in our New Testament in the letters called First and Second Corinthians.

The troubles in Macedonia were the usual— the Jewish Christians and the Law, the Greek converts who thought that baptism meant they could stop all personal effort to be holy and do whatever they pleased.

Paul spent the rest of the summer making his tour of the churches of Macedonia—churches in the cites of Thessalonica, Philippi, and Berea.

At last, in A. D. 55, Paul reached Corinth.

Chapter 4/*Adventuring in the Face of Danger*, A.D. 56

LOOKING AHEAD

Paul was glad to be back in Corinth, and the church welcomed him warmly. He knew, however, that he must not stay long.

Old divisions had been healed, and now there were many faithful workers in Corinth— Timothy, Lucius, Jason, Sosipater, Gaius, Erastus, Quartus, and others. For the first time in a long time, everything seemed to be running smoothly. Paul was looking ahead, making plans. In Corinth, he often heard news from the west. He heard how the church in Rome was growing, and he wanted to visit the Christians there.

He had never been to Rome. The church in Rome had been going for a long time, and Paul usually visited a city only when he wanted to start a church, or to revisit one he had already started.

A LETTER TO
THE ROMAN CHRISTIANS

Paul decided to write a letter to the church in Rome so the Christians there would understand his visit. He wanted them to know exactly what the Christian faith meant to him and what he preached. Tertius, a young Christian in Corinth, agreed to take Paul's dictation. Paul took a great deal of care in writing this long letter.

Paul greeted the Romans and began simply, "I am eager to preach the Good News to you also who live in Rome. For I have complete confidence in the gospel; it is God's power to save all who believe, first the Jews and also the Gentiles. For the gospel reveals how God puts people right with himself: It is through faith from beginning to end. As the scripture says, 'The person who is put right with God through faith shall live.' "

Paul explained what it means to be a Christian. He said that when we live by God's spirit we are God's children. And when we are his children, we share all God's riches and his suffering. He said that the Spirit will always help us, even when we don't know how to handle our daily problems ourselves, or don't even know how to pray. God sees into our hearts and understands us. We know everything that happens to us is for our good if we love God and are trying to fit into his plans.

Paul gave the Roman Christians some good, practical advice. He told them to work hard and not be lazy, to be patient when they had troubles, to remember to pray at all times, to share what they had with the needy, and to treat everybody the same way.

Paul planned to go to Rome and then on to Spain. But first he had to go to Jerusalem with the money which the churches in Macedonia and Achaia had collected for the poor in Jerusalem.

DANGER AHEAD

Paul meant to go by ship straight from Corinth to Syria on his way to Jerusalem. But suddenly he had to change his plans. A plot to kill him on the way was uncovered!

So Paul traveled by land, instead. This gave him a chance to visit old friends along the way.

Wherever he went, crowds of believers flocked to see him and listen to him preach.

Paul celebrated the Passover in Philippi. Five days later he and Luke sailed into Troas where seven men who were to travel with him were waiting. They stayed in Troas seven days.

On the first day of the week, the Christians gathered together and Paul talked with them. He talked until after midnight. There were many oil lamps in the room where Paul was speaking, and the room became very stuffy. A young man named Eutychus was sitting in the window. It was so warm and so late that he had trouble keeping his eyes open. Finally, he went fast asleep and fell out the third-story window. Everyone thought he was dead. But Paul ran down the stairs with all the speed he could summon. Paul bent over Eutychus for a moment.

Then he straightened up and told the people, "Don't be afraid. He is still alive."

Assured by Paul that everything would be all right, they returned upstairs. Paul broke bread, thanked God, and ate. Then he continued to talk and pray with his friends until daylight.

Paul said good-bye to his friends, walked across the narrow strip of land from Troas to Assos, and boarded a ship there.

The ship's first stop was Mitylene on the island of Lesbos. The day after that it came opposite the island of Chios. The third day it touched the island of Samos. The following day it came to Miletus, which is the seaport for the city of Ephesus.

MORE GOOD-BYES

Paul could not pass by his beloved Ephesians, so he sent word for the elders to meet his ship

at Miletus. Paul greeted them warmly. Then he said, "The Holy Spirit has warned me in every city that prison and trouble are ahead of me. I don't care what happens to me if I can finish my work that the Lord Jesus has given me to do, which is to declare the Good News of the grace of God. I have been among you a long time preaching the kingdom of God, and now I must say good-bye for you will not see me again."

Paul knelt and prayed. The elders wept, hugged him, and prayed for his safety. They watched his ship sail away to the south.

BRAVELY ON

The ship sailed a straight course to Cos, and the next day to Rhodes, and from there to Patara. At Patara Paul and his traveling companions found a large Phoenician ship sailing for its home port, and they boarded it. The ship came within sight of the island of Cyprus, the place Paul and Barnabas visited on their first missionary journey, but they passed it on the left and sailed on to Tyre. Here the ship unloaded freight.

Paul and his friends went ashore and stayed

with Christians in Tyre. They told Paul not to go to Jerusalem, but he paid no attention to their warnings and sailed on to Ptolemais.

At Ptolemais, Paul and Luke left the ship and went by land to Caesarea. Again Paul's friends warned him of danger in Jerusalem. But Paul said, "What are you doing, crying like this and breaking my heart? I am ready, not only to be imprisoned in Jerusalem, but even to die for the Lord Jesus."

Paul had said he wanted to be in Jerusalem on the day of Pentecost. He was eager, also, to deliver the money which had been collected for the church in Jerusalem.

So with some of the disciples from Caesarea, he set out for Jerusalem—and trouble!

TEMPLE RIOT

The Christians in Jerusalem were glad to see the missionaries again. The day after they arrived, Paul took his whole group to James, the head of the church. All the elders were present.

After greeting them, Paul told everything that God had done among the Gentiles through his ministry. When the elders heard it, they thanked God, but they added:

"You can see how things are here, Paul. There are thousands of Jews who have become believers, and they insist on keeping the old Jewish law. They have been told that you have been teaching all the Jews who live in Gentile countries to give up the law of Moses and stop following Jewish customs. They are sure to find out that you are here.

"What should you do? Listen to us. We have an idea. There are four men who have taken a vow, and according to the old Jewish law, as soon as their vow has been completed, they will shave their heads. Go with them to the temple. Shave your head too, and pay for theirs to be shaved. Then everyone will know there is no truth in the things that have been said about you, and that you, yourself, obey the law of Moses."

Paul agreed with the plan and the next day went with the men to the temple for the ceremony. This was a public announcement of his vow to offer a sacrifice seven days later.

The seven days were almost ended when some Jews from Ephesus, who had seen Paul in the temple, stirred up the crowd. They began shouting, "Men of Israel, help! This man is teaching everywhere against the temple and the Law. Besides he has brought Gentiles into the temple. He has defiled this holy place."

These men had seen Trophimus, an Ephesian Gentile Christian, with Paul in the streets. They just guessed that Paul had brought him into the temple.

RESCUE BY SOLDIERS

The crowd became excited. They grabbed Paul and dragged him out of the temple and shut the gates behind them. The crowd was bent on killing Paul. Next to the temple was a Roman fortress, and when the soldiers heard the commotion they came running out. As soon as the crowd saw the soldiers, they stopped beating Paul.

The commander of the soldiers arrested Paul and ordered him bound with double chains and taken to the Antonia fortress next to the temple.

Paul actually had to be carried up the steps of the fortress because the mob became violent again and yelled, "Away with him! Away with him!"

At the top of the steps Paul said to the commander, Claudius Lysias, "May I speak with you?"

Lysias replied, "You are speaking Greek! Then you must not be that Egyptian who stirred up a revolt some time ago and escaped into the desert with four thousand followers."

"No," said Paul. "I am a Jew from Tarsus in Cilicia which is an important city. I would like to speak to these people."

The commander agreed, and Paul stood on the steps and motioned to the crowd to be silent. They were quieted and Paul spoke to them in Hebrew. "Brothers and fathers, hear my defense," he said. When they heard him speaking in Hebrew they listened carefully.

Paul told how he had once hounded and persecuted the Christians. He repeated the story of his conversion on the road to Damascus. He recalled how he had been told by Ananias, "The God of our fathers has chosen you to know his will and to see the Messiah and hear him speak. You are to take his message everywhere, tell what you have seen and heard."

Paul continued, "Later, I came back to Jerusalem. But God told me, 'Leave Jerusalem, for I will send you far away to the Gentiles!'"

The crowd listened until Paul came to that word, *Gentiles*. Then with one voice they shouted, "Away with him! Kill him! He's not fit to live!"

PRISON AGAIN

The Roman commander wanted to find out why the crowd had become so wild. He ordered Paul whipped so he would confess his crime.

As they put him in chains, Paul said to the captain of the guard, "Is it legal for you to beat a Roman citizen who hasn't been tried?"

When the captain heard his words he dropped everything and hurried to the commander. "This man claims to be a Roman citizen," he reported. Lysias hurried back to Paul. "Is it true that you are a Roman citizen?" he asked.

"Yes," answered Paul.

"I am, too," said the commander, "and it cost me plenty!"

"I was *born* a citizen," said Paul.

Those who were about to beat Paul left in a hurry. Claudius Lysias was frightened because it was he who had ordered a Roman citizen beaten.

The next day the commander took Paul's chains off and ordered the chief priests and the Jewish Council to meet. He had Paul brought before the Council to try to find out what all the trouble was about.

Paul had a clever thought. The Council had both Sadducees and Pharisees. Paul knew how to get them arguing among themselves. He spoke loudly: "Brothers, I am a Pharisee as were my forefathers. It is because I believe in the resurrection of the dead that I am on trial."

This divided the Council. The Sadducees said there is no resurrection. The Pharisees believed in a resurrection. The scribes of the Pharisees' party jumped up and shouted, "We find nothing wrong with this man. Perhaps it was a spirit or an angel who spoke to him on the Damascus road." The Sadducees didn't believe in spirits or angels, either, and the argument became so violent that Claudius Lysias was afraid they would pull Paul apart. He ordered his soldiers to take Paul by force back to the fortress.

That night the Lord stood beside Paul and said, "Do not be afraid. As you have witnessed to me in Jerusalem, so you must witness also in Rome."

ANOTHER PLOT UNCOVERED

The next day Paul had a visitor, his nephew, the son of his sister. Paul's nephew had heard that forty strict Jews had taken a vow not to eat or to drink until they had killed Paul. Paul called one of the officers and said to him, "Take this young man to the commander. He has something important to say."

The commander listened carefully as Paul's nephew said, "Tomorrow the Jews are going to ask you to bring Paul back to the Council, pretending they want more information. Don't listen to them, for more than forty men will be hiding, waiting to kill him."

The commander warned Paul's nephew not to tell anyone and then sent him away.

The commander immediately called two of his officers and ordered: "Get two hundred soldiers ready to leave at nine o'clock. Take seventy cavalry and two hundred spearmen. Give Paul a horse to ride and get him safely to Governor Felix in Caesarea. I will write a letter to the governor."

ON TRIAL

That night Paul was moved to Caesarea, and the commander's letter was delivered to Antonius Felix, the governor.

After he had read the letter, Felix asked, "What province are you from?"

"I am from the city of Tarsus, in Cilicia," replied Paul.

"I will hear your case when your accusers get here," said Felix, and he ordered Paul imprisoned in the official palace.

Five days later the high priest came from Jerusalem with some of the elders and a lawyer, Tertullus. Tertullus made flattering talk to Felix, then stated his case. He said: "We have found this man to be a troublemaker, stirring up Jews all over the world to riots and revolts against the Roman government. He is a ringleader of the Nazarene party. He was trying to defile our temple when we arrested him. We would have judged him according to our own law except that Lysias, the commander of the troops in Jerusalem, came and took him away, demanding that he be tried by Roman law. You can know this is true just by questioning the man."

All the Jews agreed.

Felix, however, knew that the Christians were peaceful, so he stalled by saying to Paul, "I will decide your case when Lysias, the commander, comes down." He ordered Paul put into prison but with some liberty and visiting privileges.

A few days later, Felix and his wife Drusilla, who was a Jew, sent for Paul with the request: "Tell us more about the faith of Christ Jesus."

Paul talked about justice and self-control and the judgment to come. Suddenly Felix became afraid. "You may leave, for the time being," he said. "I'll call you again when I have more time."

A bribe was what he really wanted! And so he often called Paul and talked with him.

Two years later, when Porcius Festus became the new governor, Paul was still in prison.

Festus opened Paul's trial. The Jews made many serious charges against him, but they couldn't prove any of them. Festus wanted to do the Jews a favor, so he asked Paul, "Do you want to go to Jerusalem to be tried on these charges?"

A WAY TO ROME

"No!" Paul answered. "I have done no wrong to the Jews. If I have done anything that deserves the death penalty, I do not ask to escape it. But if I am innocent, then you cannot hand me over to them. I appeal to the Emperor in Rome."

Festus checked with his advisers and decided: "You have appealed to the Emperor, to the Emperor you will go!"

Soon after that, King Agrippa and his sister, Bernice, came to Caesarea. Festus asked Agrippa's advice about Paul, because he didn't have any definite charges against him to write to the emperor.

Paul was brought before Agrippa. Again Paul told the story of his life, and his vision on the road to Damascus. Paul said: "King Agrippa, I obeyed the heavenly vision, first at Damascus, then at Jerusalem, and through all the country of Judea. Then I went to the Gentiles. For this

reason the Jews arrested me in the temple and then tried to kill me.

"I know God will take care of me. I teach nothing but what the prophets and Moses said would happen—that Christ must suffer and be the first to rise from the dead, so that he would bring light to both Jews and Gentiles."

Festus interrupted, "Paul, you are mad. Your great learning has made you insane."

"I am *not* insane, most excellent Festus, but I am speaking the truth. King Agrippa knows all these things, and I speak frankly to him because these events were not hidden away in a corner. King Agrippa, do you believe the prophets? I know you do . . ."

Agrippa interrupted, "You think you can make me a Christian in such a short time?"

Paul said, "Whether a short time or a long time, I would to God that not only you but everybody here today might become what I am—except, of course, for these chains."

The king, the governor, Bernice, and all the others with them left the room. As they left, they agreed, "This man has done nothing to deserve death or imprisonment."

Agrippa said to Festus, "He could be set free if he had not appealed to the Emperor. He will have to be sent to Rome."

Chapter 5/ *The Adventure Ends, A.D. 59–61 (or 64)*

STORM AT SEA

Paul and several other prisoners, in the custody of an officer of the imperial guard named Julius, were put aboard ship on the first stage of their journey to Rome. Luke and Aristarchus accompanied Paul.

The ship sailed north from Caesarea to Sidon, then went between the island of Cyprus and the mainland to the city of Myra. Here the prisoners changed to an Alexandrian ship bound for Italy. The ship carried passengers and a load of grain.

It was autumn and the seas were rough and the winds strong. The captain sailed the ship down the sheltered side of the island of Crete.

With great difficulty he brought the ship to a harbor called Fair Havens.

Paul knew a great deal about ships and storms. He had been shipwrecked three times and understood the dangers of travel at that time of the year. He advised not going on until spring. "We have lost much time already because of the weather," he said. "It is now October and becoming more and more dangerous to put to sea. If we do not remain here for the winter, we are likely to have injury and loss, not only of the cargo and ship, but also of our lives."

The captain and the owner of the ship, however, felt they should go on and try to reach a city called Phoenix and put in there for the winter. Phoenix had a sheltered harbor where they would be safe from storms. It would be about a twelve-hour voyage along the rocky coast.

A gentle south wind blew up, and this seemed to prove the advantage of going on. They weighed anchor and sailed along Crete, close to the shore.

But the gentle south wind was a "weather breeder." A heavy windstorm came across the land. The force of the winds and waves was tremendous. The captain tried to bring the ship back to shore, but the large vessel was unable to face such a wind and was driven before it.

It sailed along the lee or southside of a small island called Cauda. The wind and the driving rain and waves were so violent that the sailors began to secure the ship. They brought aboard the small boat usually lashed to the stern of the ship above the water level. This was a long hard job, for the ship was pitching wildly and the little boat was already filled with water.

The ship was taking a terrible beating from the waves and the shifting cargo. To reinforce the ship and protect it from the unusual pressure of the waves the sailors fastened ropes tight around the ship.

The crew was afraid the wind was taking them to the fearful sandbars off the north African coast, so they lowered the sail and let the ship drift in the wind.

The next day they began to toss the cargo overboard. The third day of the storm, the crew, aided by the passengers, threw away the tackle, baggage, and furniture.

This was a storm of hurricane force! Even the sailors were lost, because there was neither sun nor stars to sight from. For thirteen days the ship was storm-tossed.

All hope of being saved was gone. All on board became so downhearted they lost their appetites.

After they went without food for a long time, Paul came forward and said, "Men, you should have listened to me and should not have set sail from Crete. But take heart. Only the ship will be lost. Tonight an angel of God appeared to me and said, 'Paul, you must stand before Caesar. You and those with you will be saved.' I have faith in God. I'm sure we will be saved, but the ship will have to run onto some island."

On the fourteenth night—the boat was still drifting—the sailors thought they heard waves crashing against shore. They measured the depths several times and realized that the water was so shallow they were in danger of crashing on the rocks.

They let out four anchors from the stern and prayed for daylight to come.

The sailors started to lower the small row-boat into the sea, pretending to lay out anchors from the bow. Paul, alert as anybody on the vessel, realized this was a plot to escape. The anchors could not be cast from the bow or else the ship would have sunk below the waters as it swung around. Paul told Julius and the soldiers, "Unless these men stay in the ship, you cannot be saved." The soldiers cut away the ropes of the boat and let it go.

Just before dawn, Paul begged everyone to eat. "You need food for strength. Not a hair of your heads will be lost!" He gave thanks to God in the presence of all as he broke the hardtack (biscuits) and began to eat.

His manner made everyone feel better, and they all ate. When they had eaten, they lightened the ship by casting overboard the wheat and the rest of the cargo. The ship needed to ride as high in the water as possible, since it had to sail as near as it could to land when the ropes were cut.

SHIPWRECK

At early dawn the land they saw was not familiar, but they noticed a bay with a beach on which they decided to bring the ship ashore. They cast off the anchors and left them in the sea, at the same time loosening the ropes that tied the steering oars (rudders). They hoisted the foresail to the wind, and the steermen made for the beach.

They ran aground on a sandbar. The bow struck and the stern was broken up by the surf.

The soldiers were about to kill all the prisoners to keep them from escaping. Julius wanted to save Paul, so he commanded an orderly abandoning of the ship. Those who could swim threw themselves overboard first and made for land. The rest hung on to planks or pieces of the ship. When the roll was called every one of the men was safely on shore!

The island turned out to be Malta, about eighty miles south of Sicily. The people who lived there were friendly and started a bonfire for the cold, wet, tired men.

Paul was helping gather wood for the fire when a snake bit him on the hand. The people thought, "This man must be a murderer. He escaped from the sea, but he is going to be punished just the same."

Paul shook the snake into the fire, and nothing happened to him. The people then thought he was a god!

They were not far from the estate of Publius, the Roman representative on the island. He took in the weary travelers and made them feel welcome.

Three days later Publius' father was sick with fever. Paul visited him and prayed. He put his hands on the father's head and the fever left him. The rest of the people on the island who were sick also began to come to Paul. And they were cured.

The people on the island gave Paul and his friends many gifts.

Three months later the prisoners sailed from Malta on another Alexandrian ship which had wintered in the island. It bore the figurehead of the "twin gods," Castor and Pollux, favorite gods of seamen.

The ship stopped at Syracuse on the southeast coast of the island of Sicily, then circled around to Rhegium at the foot of Italy. The next day a good south wind brought them, two days later, into Puteoli, one hundred thirty miles away from Rome. Here Paul found Christians who wished to entertain him for a week.

ROME AT LAST

The rest of the trip was made on foot over the famous road called the Appian Way.

Forty miles outside of Rome, at the Forum or Market of Appius, some of the younger men of the church came out to meet Paul. At Three Taverns, a town thirty miles from Rome, another group met him. These men had probably heard about the letter he had written to the

Roman church. Paul was so touched that he thanked God and renewed his courage.

In Rome, Paul was allowed to live by himself, but he was always guarded by a soldier.

Three days after his arrival, Paul called together the local Jewish leaders and spoke to them. "I want you to know," he said, "that I am in prison, not as a criminal, but as one who appealed to Caesar. It is because I believe the Messiah has come that I am bound with this chain."

The Jewish leaders said, "We have heard nothing against you. No letters or reports have come from Judea. We want to hear what you believe, for the only thing we know about Christians is that they are opposed everywhere."

A time was set, and on that day a large group came. Paul told them about the kingdom of God. He used the Scripture—the five Law books of Moses, and the books of the prophets—to teach them about Jesus. He began preaching in the morning and went on into the evening!

Some of the people were convinced by Paul's words, but others did not believe. They left, disagreeing among themselves.

For two years Paul lived in a rented house. He had many visitors and always told them bluntly about the kingdom of God and the Lord Jesus Christ, and no one tried to stop him.

Restless, active Paul was now a prisoner for Christ! He wrote to the Philippians, "I have learned to be satisfied in whatever condition I find myself."

PAUL'S DEATH

When did Paul die? How did he die? Our Bible does not say. Some people think that after two years in prison he was released and went on to visit Spain, and that three years later during violent persecution of the Christians, he was killed. Tradition says that it was during this persecution of the church by the Emperor Nero in A.D. 64 that Paul was sentenced to death and beheaded.

A Blessing from Paul

"The grace of the Lord Jesus Christ and the love of God and the fellowship of the Holy Spirit be with you all"
(II Cor. 13:14).

Chapter 6/*An Afterword for Parents and Teachers*

LETTERS!

How were they collected? Who knew where to look for them? No one knows for sure. It could be that someone remembered Paul had written several letters to the Christians in Corinth, or had heard him dictating a letter to the Galatians, or remembered that Paul had written a letter to a slave owner, Philemon. What if these letters could be found and shared?

Maybe this question started a search. No one knows for sure. But we do know that some letters were preserved, letters Paul had written to the Colossians, the Galatians, the Thessalonians, the Philippians, the Corinthians, and the Romans. And there was that very personal letter to Philemon, the slave owner.

One letter was meant for all Christians. It was addressed simply to the church. Later it became known as the letter to the Ephesians. No one is sure Paul wrote the letter. He might have written it from the prison in Rome about the same time that he wrote a letter to the Colossian Christians. If Paul didn't write it, some faithful Christian wrote in it Paul's name and included some of the main ideas from each of Paul's letters. He especially used the letter to the Colossians which was one of Paul's last letters. Both Colossians and Ephesians were written to help the church and individual Christians understand God's plan for them.

Letters were found addressed to Timothy and Titus, written in Paul's name. These letters had in them ideas and messages from Paul.

It was important to the early Christians to know what Paul said so they could remember what it means to be a Christian.

PAUL SPEAKS TODAY

Paul's letters were not just for a few people who lived long ago. They are for all Christians in all times.

Paul had two main ideas he wanted all Christians to understand.

First—Christ Must Dominate Our Lives

Many things can easily dominate our lives— TV, money, ourselves, trying to get all we can, and many others. But Paul said a Christian can't be dominated by these things. He wrote: "Do not conform yourselves to the standards of this world, but *let God transform you inwardly* by a complete change of your mind. Then you will be able to know the will of God—what is good and is pleasing to him and is perfect . . . . Do not think of yourself more highly than you should" (Rom. 12:2-3 TEV, italics added).

"Get rid of your old self. . . . Your hearts and minds must be made completely new, and you must put on the new self, which is created in God's likeness and reveals itself in the true life that is upright and holy. . . .

"Get rid of all bitterness, passion, and anger. No more shouting or insults, no more hateful feelings of any sort. Instead, be kind and tender-hearted to one another, and forgive one another, as God has forgiven you through Christ. . . .Your life must be controlled by love" (Eph. 4:22-24, 31; 5:2 TEV).

Paul told what it means to let Christ's love control your life. He wrote: "If I speak in the tongues of men and of angels, but have not love, I am a noisy gong or a clanging cymbal. And if I have prophetic powers, and understand all mysteries and all knowledge, and if I have all faith, so as to remove mountains, but have not love, I am nothing. If I give away all I have, and if I deliver my body to be burned, but have not love, I gain nothing.

"Love is patient and kind; love is not jealous or boastful; it is not arrogant or rude. Love does not insist on its own way; it is not irritable or resentful; it does not rejoice at wrong, but rejoices in the right. Love bears all things, believes all things, hopes all things, endures all things.

"Love never ends. . . . So faith, hope, love abide, these three; but the greatest of these is love" (I Cor. 13:1-8*a*, 13).

Paul not only wanted people to remember that first *Christ must dominate our lives*, but—

Second—We Are All One in Christ

When we follow Christ, we are no longer divided into groups—black or white, Indians or Africans, Asians or Americans. We are a family of God. We are *one* in Christ.

Paul said the church—all Christians—is like a body. A body has different kinds of parts—feet, hands, arms, a head. Each part has something special to do. Each part isn't the body, but all the parts together make the body. Individual Christians are like parts of a body. All are needed to make up the body.

Paul wrote: "Christ is like a single body, which has many parts; it is still one body, even though it is made up of different parts. . . . There would not be a body if it were all only one part! . . . And so there is no division in the body, but all its different parts have the same concern for one another. If one part of the body suffers, all the other parts suffer with it; if one part is praised, all the other parts share its happiness.

"All of you, are Christ's body, and each one is a part of it" (I Cor. 12:12, 19, 25-27 TEV).

Important Words

Abba—An Aramaic word meaning "father."

Apostle—A person who is sent forth, a messenger, the first twelve followers of Jesus who spread the word about him.

Ceremony—An order or way of doing something, especially formal.

Ceremonies—Religious customs.

Convert—A person whose beliefs have been changed.

Conversion—The process of changing.

Disciple—A learner or follower.

Elders—Respected religious leaders or church officers.

Famine—Extreme scarcity of food often leading to starvation.

Gentile—A person who is not a Jew.

Grace—God's great love for man which cannot be earned, but which is offered by God as a free gift.

Idols—Representations of a god made of wood, or stone, or metal, and worshiped by people.

Judaizers—People who wanted to convert everyone to the Jewish religion. They thought Christians should also practice Jewish customs.

The Law—The collection of rules and regulations followed by the Jews in their religion. They were based on the first five books of the Old Testament.

Missionaries—People who have a "mission" or special work to do. Paul had a special work or "calling" to preach the Good News about Jesus to the Gentiles.

Pagan—Someone who is not a Christian or Jew.

Persecuted—Made to suffer because of religious beliefs or practices.

Persecutor—The one who persecutes.

Passover—An important spring festival celebrating the deliverance of the Hebrews from Egyptian slavery. This is an important Jewish religious festival.

Pentecost—A harvest festival coming in late May or early June when the Jews offered the first fruits of their fields to God.

Pharisees—Jewish interpreters of the Mosaic Law.

Rabbi—Jewish teacher of the Law.

Reconciling—Bringing agreement between persons who have had a misunderstanding, making persons friends again.

Sadducees—A religious party of the Jews made up mostly of priests. The high priest of the temple was chosen from among them.

Scribes—In New Testament times, a group of men who taught and defended the Law.

Spiritual Gifts—Those abilities a person discovers he has when he lives close to God. See Galatians 5:22-23.

Stoning—A method of execution where stones were thrown at the victim until he was dead.

Temple—The great sacred building in Jerusalem that was the religious center of the Jews.

Speaking in Tongues—An emotional experience in which a person is considered possessed by the Holy Spirit and utters sounds that often cannot be understood.

Witness—Someone who has firsthand knowledge of a fact or an event.